TRUE HOSPITAL GHOST STORIES

A collection of paranormal events from the staff who experienced them

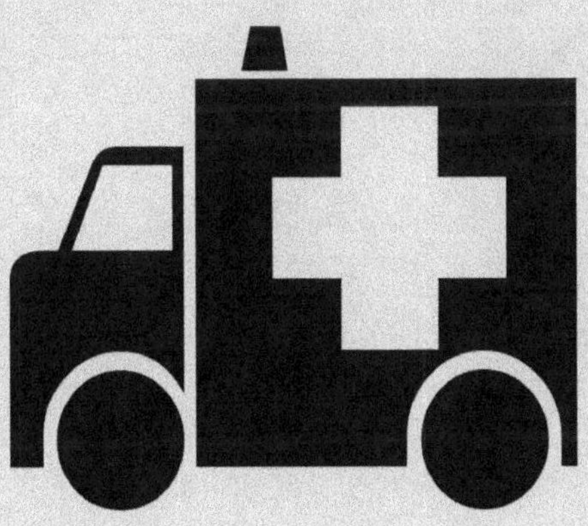

By John Stancil

Hospitals are places of life and death. Every day, every minute, every hour, someone is born and someone else dies in a hospital. These are structures which could be seen as gateways to and from life.

After having my own paranormal encounter as a teenager, I've always had a fascination with life after death. Even as a young kid, I was wholly fascinated by ghost stories. In college, I formed a team of paranormal investigators and ghost hunted with them.

I decided for this simple effort to investigate and collect the true stories, accounts from the individuals who experienced them, of paranormal events occuring in hospitals. These men and women see death on an almost daily basis, and sometimes the echoes of the deceased linger after their passing.

> Death is but a door,
> Time is but a window.

Enjoy,
John S.

PIGTAILS

I was a young nurse at our hospital, having been there for just a few months.

I had taken a woman up to day surgery from the emergency room for an endoscopy, and they called me back down and asked me to get her family up as well, as she only spoke Italian, and not enough English, and they wanted someone to agree to the operation.

I went past the waiting room and down the hall to the elevators after dropping them off. I took the back way to the ER, and the hallways are abandoned – this used to be the pediatric wing of the hospital, but it has been closed for years, and the rooms are now vacant and cluttered with broken equipment, chairs, and other junk.

When I approached the old nurses station at the T intersection of the pediatric hallway and the corridor leading to the elevators, I saw a small child standing across from the nurses station further down the hall. She had large pigtails, a brown shirt, white sneakers, and was hugging a teddy bear. I assumed she was a relative who had come out of the day surgery waiting room. I was afraid she would enter one of the rooms and get injured or disoriented, so I asked, "Honey, what are you doing? You don't need to be out there. You're going to get hurt." I went around the nursing station to reach over and take her wrist, bringing her inside.

I kid you not, she vanished when I approached her from about ten feet away.

Every hair on my body stood up straight, and I turned and raced down to the elevator like a bat out of hell. I hammered the button incessantly before the elevator reached the building. When I approached the nurses station, white as a mask, one of the senior nurses stared at me and asked, "What's wrong with you?"

I recall babbling like a fool as I attempted to explain what had happened. After a few moments of listening to me, the nurse said, "Oh, you saw the little girls ghost. She's been a fixture around here for years" and I recall saying, "Well, thank you for informing me about it prior to this."

According to reports, the ghost has been seen down in the emergency department, ducking in and out of patient rooms and peering under curtained areas. My wife operated on the seventh floor and she said that one night, a whole row of patient rooms began screaming about a small child running through the rooms.

Lucy Barron - Hoffman Estates, IL

AS IF THEY WERE LEAVING

I work in a small community hospital in intensive care. Our 9-bed unit is totally isolated from the medical floor by two doorways. We were all charting when we heard footsteps come down the hallway. It's an entirely open unit from which you can see into any room.

We were the only people in the unit. CT is below us, and they close at 5 PM, unless there is an emergency, and we only have people on the second floor. The third floor is used for storage, so there was no one above us. This occurred two or three times.

Then, in the two empty rooms, cupboard doors kept opening and closing. When I finally asked my co-worker what was going on, she simply stated that it is a common occurrence following someone's death, especially if it was unexpected.

Roselyn Getchell - Rainier, OR

STRIPED SHIRT

We were discussing a patient's hallucinations when a coworker told me about this time he was walking past a patient's bed, an elderly woman with dementia, who was engaged in animated conversation with someone.

When I inquired as to who she was speaking with, she responded, "The sweet guy in the black and white striped shirt." I then entered another patient's dementia bed, where the other patient inquired as to where the man in the striped shirt had gone.

Roy Wilcox - Hopkins, MN

THAT BLACK THING UP THERE

I've heard from a nurse that she was floated to oncology at the hospital where she previously worked one night. She was entrusted with a dying patient who had been unconscious for several days. At one point during the night, the nurse entered the room and found the patient at the top of the bed, looking at her and saying, "Don't let them take me!" The nurse was terrified and inquired as to who was going to take her, to which she replied, "That black thing up there" while pointing upward in the air. This patient died moments later.

Dana Mullins - San Luis Obispo, CA

STRANGE SHAPE

I was caring for a dying male patient one night. He was terrified, and I spent a considerable amount of time with him, attempting to calm and comfort him. He eventually settled down, and I stepped away from the bedside to the nurses station, which was about fifteen feet away. As I sat, I cast my gaze over to him and noticed a shadowy figure standing over the bed, staring down at the patient. I was afraid, and I'm certain it was something malicious.

Katherine Ball - West Palm Beach, FL

I previously worked in a state institution for developmentally disabled individuals. We were temporarily moved to another building when our building was undergoing renovations. In any case... I was working second shift one night.

We had a locked pica unit. I saw one of the residents strolling down the corridor. Quite distinctive gait and very distinct yellow t-shirt emblazoned with a smiling face. I entered the ward to inform workers that they were dealing with an escapee. This was a serious situation, as this particular resident, Gary, would consume literally everything from clothes to pens to plastic. He was also adamant about returning to his home ward which is why I did not bring him back myself. He would have needed two escorts. When we returned to the hall, Gary had vanished in less than five seconds. We combed the whole structure. He was nowhere to be found outside, downstairs, or in any of the wards. This entire search took longer than ten minutes due to the fact that I had all extra workers searching for him.

I was just about to call the house supervisor to let her know that we "lost" someone when out from the bathroom walks Gary with one of the staff. He had been getting his bath in the bathroom for the last thirty minutes or so. I absolutely, without a doubt, saw

Gary in the hallway. I never would've short staffed the wards like I did if I hadn't seen him. Like I said, very distinctive gait, look, and clothing. They all thought that I was crazy.

I later came to find out the next day, after the story goes around that I am crazy, that Gary had an identical twin brother who died in that building three years previously.

Evelyn Nims - Hattiesburgh, MS

We had an African American child, about ten years old, in the intensive care unit after she sustained serious injuries in a car accident. She suffered numerous injuries to the brain. She did not die there, but was transferred weeks later to another hospital.

Following that, I am aware of three older African American males in their fifties who, if even slightly sedated, would inquire about the small girl with the ribbon in her hair sitting at the foot of their beds.

"She asked me how I was doing, then got up and went that way," one gentleman explained, pointing to the second floor doors. He paused, a wide-eyed expression crossing his face, and then continued, "But I suppose she couldn't have left the room that way, huh?"

Personally, I believe she was entrusted with the treatment of grandfather figures.

Joseph Pritchard - Clarks Hill, IN

MURDERER'S ROOM

I worked in an intensive care unit where an inmate
accused of murder died in ICU 1 – and nobody would
bring another patient in that room after that due
to the air being too dense and the room being too
spooky and dark.

The situation became so severe that the hospital finally closed the room and demolished a wall to create a
new entrance to the unit, as nurses refused to admit
patients even though it was the last available bed.
They'd triage a patient before placing them in that
bed.

Shirley Scott - San Antonio, TX

OLD NURSE

I was working in the NICU at the time of a tornado attack. Several nurses were recalled to help with the emergency plan at a sister hospital in town. When it was all said and done, one of the nurses returned with the following story: She was assisting the nurses in administering some medications prior to herding everybody into the hallways. Each patient she visited said that they had already received their medications from the sweet nurse in the white uniform and hat. After she left, she remembered that it had been a long time since a nurse wore a hat.

The story established the Old Nurse urban legend. According to the story, she had an affair with a married physician, became pregnant, and then consented to him performing an abortion on her in the 2nd floor OR bed. She died, and he was arrested. She was never discharged from the hospital and was often seen. Every year around Halloween, the local newspaper will run an article about her sightings. The hospital has since been demolished and replaced by college dormitories. I'm curious as to if any students have seen her.

Ann Wells - Birmingham, AL

MARY

We closed room 3 in our MICU after nearly every pa-tient since Mary's death reported seeing a woman in a white habit rocking back and forth by their bedside. Apparently, this nun never makes eye contact, she just looks out the window, directly above their head. This window looks out into the hospital graveyard, which contains the graves of deceased nuns.

Mary was a nun who died in the 1950's in a car crash outside the hospital. She was approximately 30 years old, and every patient described her as a young wom-an. We were both convinced it was the "sun-down syndrome." Since then, Room 3 has been our storage room, which no one enters alone unless absolutely necessary.

Amanda Flock - Fort Lauderdale, FL

PERSISTENT

We had a guy who was a chronic CHF patient who was always on the call button and despised being on fluid restrictions. The nurses would take turns answering the call button during the shift so the primary can focus on other tasks.

He was a frequent flyer because he was very chronic, borderline, and the hospital was the only place where he did not suffer from fluid overload.

I operate from 7:00 PM to 7:00 AM. He died shortly after 8 p.m. The expression on his face, as if to say, "How could you possibly let me go!" As if it were our fault.

Family members arrived and left by 9, and the funeral home departed at 9:30.

Around 10 PM, the call button begins to sound. I was present. The call button rang every five minutes. One of the nurses was an extremely spiritual young lady. Around 2 AM, after about four hours of this, the nurse yelled "All right!"

She gets up, marches to the room and yells into the empty space, "Mr X, you have died. You are no longer able to be in here troubling us. Leave. I am exorcising you from this plane of existence in the name of Jesus.

Go into the light!"

I am not exaggerating when I say that the call button immediately stopped working.

Melissa Marcum - Saint Louis, MO

ISOLATED

This is not a horror story, just a story about a lonely ghost.

One of the rooms is fine if it is frequently used. There are no issues. However, since it was a space at the end of the hall, it was frequently used for storage.

After a few weeks with no patients/activity in the room, the call light will begin to flash four or five times per shift. However, if you entered the room and switched on the television, the call light would remain off.

As a result, when the space was being used for storage, the television was still on at a low volume.

Tony Roque - Sunrise, FL

As is the case for the majority of very old hospitals, ours was once owned by nuns. One unit had been transformed into an outpatient sleep study lab. I was watching the video monitor during one shift in the middle of the night when five patients started simultaneously removing their monitoring equipment. As I entered the first room to inquire about what was going on, the patient said that the old nurse with the cap informed her that the analysis was complete and she should leave. Each patient related the exact same story.

Mike Townsend - Southfield, MI

EKG STRIP

I work on a cardiac care unit where the majority of patients are post-heart attack. My charge nurse explained this story to us. I'm not sure if she was joking, but she sounded serious. As a result of the unit being vacant, we transferred our final couple of patients to the ICU due to the low patient census. My charge nurse was at the nurses station in the CCU, working on something on the phone.

One of our rooms was deserted. She entered the room where the noise was coming from and discovered an EKG strip coming out of the bedside printer, which we never use, which was a long continuous strip of clear V-Tach. She said that she had just coded someone there a week prior who was from Michigan.

Margarita Andrews - Vincennes, IN

As an EMT, I perform inter-facility transfers and thus get to see all of the state's qualified facilities and hospitals.

Two locations give me the creeps: an abandoned "special education school" and the state's prison mental health hospital, which used to be a major tuberculosis ward during the days of massive outbreaks.

A third unsettling location is an old birthing hospital that has been converted into a long-term care facility. The whole top floor is padlocked. I asked a nurse on the elevator, jokingly, if the building was haunted, and she responded matter-of-factly. On the top level, there are shapes resembling small children, and residents report older women wearing dresses. She mentioned that she was unable to enter some parts of the building without the company of another person.

Joshua Johnson - Pontiac, MI

NEVER OPEN THE DOOR

I would always hear banging coming from inside the freezer in the morgue at my hospital. It was truly terrifying, particularly when the pathologist looked up, grabbed my shoulders, locked his gaze on me, and said "You hear that? When they knock, you never open the door. Absolutely never."

It was discovered to be some loose pipes, and he thought it was amusing that I didn't sleep that night.

Casey Machado - Beaumont, TX

WHO IS THAT LITTLE GIRL?

I work in a long-term care facility, which contains the legend of the little girl. Many have seen her; few have lived to tell the tale. Numerous residents have inquired, "Who is that little girl" and pointed to her. These people, coincidentally, will die within three days of seeing her. As it turns out, about ten years ago, a fatal car accident occurred directly in front of our LTC. Who is the victim? A small child, about ten years old.

Richard Polley - Waltham, MA

ETHEL

A retired military captain and his wife, Ethel, decided to sell their home and relocate to Florida. They sold their house to the state, which intended to use it as a resident home for mentally ill teenagers.

Ethel died in the house after the closing.

Residents often made reference to the "old woman" they saw on a daily basis. The nursing staff referred to her simply as "Ethel."'

Late at night, while the residents were sleeping, if the staff changed the channel to more adult content, the television would turn off and restart on a different channel.

There was this one nurse who believed the whole house was plotting her demise. She'd swear that she was tripped by the carpet. When cupboards were opened, knives aimed directly at her would fall out. It turns out that this nurse was ultimately terminated for assaulting and stealing from patients.

Ethel looks after her "children."

Noel Kennon - Owensburg IN

JOAN

I serve as a certified nursing assistant in long term care. We had one resident named "Joan" who was completely self-sufficient; she performed all ADL's on her own and did well on her own; she never had an incident. She requested assistance only during showers, and then to ensure she did not slip and fall. Joan developed pneumonia and was hospitalized. When she returned, she was too frail to do it on her own but too stubborn to seek assistance. Before she went to bed, the CNA told her, "If you want to get up, hit your call light. I'll come assist you." Naturally, she did not, disabling the bed alarm, climbing out of bed and falling. Joan died as a result of the fall. Following that, no one was put into bed C (Joan's bed).

The next week, the room's call light was turned on at night. I walked down to the place, assuming it was the resident in bed B, to see what she desired. When I entered the room, I noticed that while the call lights for beds B and A were turned off, the call light for bed C (Joan's unoccupied bed) was turned on. My eyes welled up with tears, and I retreated from the room, directing someone else to switch off the call light.

Larry Gutierrez - Denton, TX

INSPECTOR

We have an individual whom we refer to as the inspector. He reappears at the far end of the long corridor, as our wings are L shaped. He is holding a clipboard. When he appears, the resident normally dies within a couple of days. Additionally, residents have contacted us to inform us that a man was standing next to their roommate's bed and that we should inform him to leave as per our policy of no men on nights. Usually, the roommate dies shortly afterwards. Then there's the matter of the girls.

Several coherent residents have mentioned seeing little girls in the hallways at night. We are directly behind a children's home where children have been abused in the past.

Becky Smith - Elkin, NC

VIRGIL, YOU'RE HERE FOR ME.

As I had done for years, I was working a night shift as an aide caring for a lady with terminal cancer on hospice at home. She was beginning to falter, and I roused her family, two daughters and DH. We were all seated, and she was very quiet and serene. She abruptly turned toward the door and said, "Virgil, Virgil, you're here for me. I'm prepared, and they're not going to let me go." I saw a shadowy figure enter the room and felt the creepiest evil sensation. I'm not easily scared, but I was relieved when it was time for me to return home. I turned to observe this spirit, and my family looked at me as if to say, "What are you looking at?"

Later that day, the lady died.

A few months later, her daughter became ill, but not terminally ill, and they contacted my agency to see if I could come and stay with her at night for a few days while she recovered. I spent two nights there. The house is filled with strange paranormal activity. Voices in empty rooms, the sound of people moving about while everyone was sleeping, and so on. I determined that regardless of how ill she was or how much that family adored me, I would not work another shift there.

Elizabeth Greene - Stamford, CT

In bed 3, there was a transient patient named "Willy" who was kept alive for approximately three months due to modern medicine, with no family to stop care. Willy died, but patients in bed 3 frequently speak of their friend Willy, who gave them a blanket or stopped by to chat. Bed 3 is located at the unit's end and features an ante room. If you are in the ante room or viewing the room on the monitor, you cannot see directly into Bed 3. One night when there was no patient in Bed 3, the monitor switched to the room and a body was seen lying over the side of the bed, over the side rails, floating in a way. The room was searched and found to be empty.

Another night, a nurse who has operated on the unit for a few years noticed someone sitting cross-legged in a chair behind the door to Bed 3. She was perplexed as to how a family member gained access to the room given our restricted visiting hours. She entered the room and discovered that it was deserted. Needless to say, she was terrified.

Additionally, there was another patient who was a young woman in her twenties who contracted necrotizing facilitis from one of her children who was infected with strep. She spent some time in the unit and finally died. As one of the new nurses arrived on the next shift inquired as to why the patient was standing on the backside of the unit holding her twin daughters' hands, wondering how she had made such a remarkable recovery, she was told that the patient had died earlier that day.

Paul Ruiz - Hollister, CA

FIRST DEATH

It was a newly renovated four-bedroom unit. Around 3 a.m., I was monitoring the screens and listening to the patient snore. The pencil drawer slid open, and I didn't think much about it because the hospital was on a very busy avenue and I assumed it was caused by vibrations from the busy road below. After several attempts at sliding the drawer shut, I decided that if the drawer felt the need to be open, so be it.

I heard a noise in the room several minutes later: the patient's bathroom door opening and the sound of someone moving an IV pole. Since I couldn't see the bathroom clearly, I assumed one of the staff members from the first floor had rushed in to wash their hands. I raised my eyes from my monitor viewing to observe a patient who had just been admitted to the unit. Mrs. G, an elderly woman who presented with unusual chest pain, developed sepsis as a result of a gallbladder problem. She had apparently died in the unit.

Although the hospital had been on this site for years, the unit had been completely demolished, including taking down walls and replacing them. I heard the patient's bathroom door open, and I heard the IV pole rattling and shuffling feet once more. I raised my eyes and saw Mrs. G. standing in the center of the room, one hand moving the IV pole and the other resting on top of the pole's pump. She came to a halt, turned and waved, shook her head as if to assure everyone that everything would be fine, took a few steps, and vanished.

It was quite the sight to behold. Immediately after that vision, one of the floor's nurses came in to see if I needed something. I told her that I was fine. And inquired as to whether she had ever seen a ghost in the hospital. She stared at me, gasped, and inquired "No, why?" I explained what had just occurred to her. She declared she would never return to that room.

Mrs. G was the unit's first death. She was well-liked by the entire team, and I had the distinct impression that she was keeping an eye on us. When the day shift arrived, I told them my story. They were not taken aback. When I worked at various hospitals and as a Nurse Extern during my senior year of nursing school and heard older nurses say ghost stories, I assumed they were just burned out.

Thomas Bell - Denver, CO

BLOODBATH

I was working my usual night shift with one other nurse in a bone marrow transplant unit. We had five patients, and the time was about 3:30 a.m. My co-worker had just emerged from room 4, and as she came around the corner, I startled her. She was emptying a urinal when the bathroom door closed on her, which freaked her out and resulted in her spilling urine on herself.

She then continued to inform me that there had been a young gentleman in that room who had died a very grisly death.

Apparently, this gentleman was scheduled to return home, but one night around 4:00 AM, the nurses heard a thump; the sound of a person collapsing.

They hurried into the room and discovered this guy in the shower, central line disconnected, and blood all over. They attempted to code him, but he died immediately in the bathroom. Nobody knows why he pulled his line or what happened, but the scene was clearly a bloodbath.

A few weeks later, a sweet little old lady enters the room and inquires of the nurse whether anyone has died in it. The nurse clarified that this was a hospital and that it was possible for anyone to die. According

to the woman, "I believe a young man died here."
When the nurse inquires why, the lady answers,
"Because he's speaking to me." This lady has a tri-
ple lumen central line. Later, when the nurse enters,
there is blood everywhere. One of her lines has been
snipped. Not extracted, just sliced. The room is devoid
of scissors. The lady states that "He did it."

Charles Hoekstra - Waco, TX

WHITE UNIFORM

I am a registered nurse from South Africa now resid-
ing and working in Ohio. When I was working Night
Shift in South Africa, the strangest thing happened
to me one night. I had a patient who I suspected
was messing with his IV, which caused me a slew of
headaches. After having to open the clamp for what
felt like the hundredth time that night, I questioned
him. He became enraged with me and said he had
done nothing wrong but instead blamed it on a young
nurse in a white gown who he said had fiddled with
it repeatedly. I was perplexed because we in South
Africa wear special uniforms and they were not white
at this particular hospital. Needless to say, I was
enraged, and I believe we both left the conversation
exasperated.

I had forgotten about his story about the young nurse
for several weeks before I found myself in a completely different room with a completely different patient
one night. The call light rang, and when I went to answer it, the patient informed me that he was having
an issue with one of my staff members. I inquired as
to what. He said that a young nurse dressed in white
stood silently in the doorway of the dark bathroom,
looking at him, which freaked him out. My hair stood
on end at this point, but I told him that he was probably dreaming and checked the bathroom just to be
certain. There was nothing there, but it is something I

can never forget.

Another case involved a patient in a private room who was terminally ill with liver cancer. I worked days, but night shift employees complained that they despised entering the room because something would blow on the back of their necks and shadows would pass where they shouldn't be. The man and his wife were both Christians, and his wife said that she witnessed this black presence descend over him and cause his breathing to become labored. She requested that I and a friend pray for her, which we gladly did as Christians. We blessed and anointed the room, prayed with the family, and prayed for the Lord to seal the room. From that point on, the room was filled with harmony and affection, and the man's breathing became much easier. There were no longer any objections to entering. This gentle little man passed away finally, still in a state of peace and affection.

Mike Parsons - Toledo, OH

VOODOO

For the last four years, I've worked as a night nurse in an elderly care facility. I had a palliative who was unable to sleep due to very vivid hallucinations. She described voodoo people surrounding her room, simply staring at her, waiting for her to die. I didn't take it seriously until the lady across the hall began seeing them in her room as well.

Amber Miller - Mount Pleasant, TX

HISSING CAT

I operate in a cardio surgical intensive care unit. Our unit receives a high volume of messed up individuals both physically and mentally. We had a period of nights during which each corner room in our unit, which is a perfect square, where patients reported seeing a cat.

Apparently, he is not a sweet cat either. The creature hissed at them. We spent probably a half hour searching for a cat and then had security/plan operators come look as well. No cat has ever been seen or discovered. Two of those four patients coded the next day.

Albert Small - Taylors Falls, MN

On the night shift, I work on a stroke/telemetry floor. The majority of our patients are senior citizens. Apparently, patients see two things before they die.

Some would say that two men enter their rooms and inform them that they must prepare to leave. The patient will contact us and inform us that these men are large and have an abrasive disposition. When they see the two guys, they are either frightened or irritated. Additionally, they can see a small child enter their rooms and attempt to awaken them. Typically, the boy is boisterous and races around their room. Patients will call and inquire as to who is allowing children to roam freely late at night.

Several nights or even the same night, we're coding the patient or cleaning the patient in preparation for pick up by the funeral home.

Lynda Taylor - Wheeling, WV

FINGERPRINTS

My town is home to two very old hospitals. One ceases to operate overnight, and the reports are disturbing. Nobody cleans the old emergency room alone, as all lights and call bells are turned off. Other floors feature a child with a ball, a lady in a white gown, and so forth.

A coworker was cleaning an entire floor independently, as is customary, and bouncing between rooms due to the cleaning solution being wet for a few minutes. As I returned to a freshly wiped room, I could clearly see tiny hand prints.

Andrea Forrester - Little Rock, AR

DO NOT LET ME GO BACK

When my mother operated as an emergency room nurse, she saw a man who had been involved in a car accident and was bleeding profusely. The man jolted awake during resuscitation and cried, "Do not let me go back there! Do not let me go back!" They lost him a few seconds later.

Nellie Dutra - Lansing, MI

CALL LIGHT

As a nurse's assistant, I work midnight shifts in a long-term care hospital. I was responsible for one guy, who was unable to use his call light.

He had serious dementia and crippling Parkinson's disease, but his light was still looped around the railing of his bed. His light came on one night, and I went to answer it, already perplexed and creeped out. I switched it off. The light came back on before I could get out of the room. When I returned, I discovered that the light had been unplugged from the wall and thrown underneath his covers. I fished it out, reconnected it, and walked away.

I saw shadows standing over me and felt a hard tap on my shoulder when performing chest compressions on the man a few nights later, he died within minutes.

Dorothy Slick - Dumas, AR

One night in Iraq, I was working a guard shift in the CHS on the FOB. Since there had been no activity for the previous week, the workforce was completely asleep. As I walked through the halls, I noticed that everything was supposed to be turned off or on standby. I walked past a room that they used to house traumatized locals. I toggled the button down to turn off the lights. I resumed my walk down the hall and noticed out of the corner of my eye that the lights had been restored. This is when I activated my alarm system. I stepped around the corner and took a look around the place. There was nothing.

I flipped the switch back to the down position and walked over to the intercom. The radio was malfunctioning. As a result, I started walking back to the CQ desk to personally report it. The lights were restored. I'm a bit on edge at the moment. I am unable to radio for assistance, there is no one on this side of the compound who can hear me scream, and the light switch location constantly changes when the lights are turned back on. Bear in mind that I am currently assigned to a Forward Operating Base in a battle zone. When I went to clear the corner and look into the room again, all I saw was an empty room, a gurney, a heart monitor, and a crash cart.

I couldn't tell you why I said what I said to this day,

but I was afraid that if I didn't, the lights would continue to turn on. "If you're afraid of the dark," I said, "I'll leave the light on."

I completed my shift and turned off the light. I left a note on the desk stating that one of the surgeons had requested that I always keep the light on in case of an emergency. The light had stayed on throughout the remainder of my shifts.

Jordan Byrd - New York, NY

WHISTLER

For a couple of years, I worked in a hospital as a transporter. The transport home base was located in the hospital's basement, which is also where all laundry and supplies are sorted. I despised working late nights in the aftermath of this incident.

I was alone in the basement on this particular night when I heard whistling at the end of the hallway near the elevator. I peered around the corner, hoping to see my sole coworker on duty that evening, but there was nobody there. I brushed it aside; I am not easily frightened. Since evenings are sluggish, I snacked and hung out in the break room for a while. I then hear a loud boom. When I entered the hallway, I saw a bed rolling down the corridor, bumping into the walls.

At this point, I believe my coworker is deceiving me. When I radio him, he responds that he is upstairs in the cafeteria.

I still didn't believe him and believe I'll catch him red-handed. As I walked past the laundry room, the machines began to operate. I poked my head in, hoping to see him, but it's totally deserted. I'm beginning to feel anxious. When I entered the laundry room, the machines came to a complete halt. When I heard whistling again, I froze, then ran out and into the elevator. At this point, I am aware that I am the sole employee in the basement.

As I wait for the elevator, items began to fall from the shelves down the corridor. Glove boxes, tissue boxes, tube bundles, I was standing there watching them slide to the opposite end of the hallway one by one. I swear, my whole body broke out in goosebumps, my hair stood on end, and I had this strong gut feeling that I was being watched, that I was not alone.

As I entered the elevator, I felt as if someone was brushing my shoulder. I went upstairs and discovered my coworker in the cafeteria, completely freaked out. I got out of there and was quickly moved. To add to the creepiness, I always whistle mindlessly to myself at work; it was almost as if the spirit was imitating me. The most terrifying sensation imaginable.

Naomi Lovett - Higginsville, MO

SCREAMING

The initial story: After a lengthy stay in CCU, where I worked at the time, we were eventually moved to the surgery floor and a patient coded. We operated on him for thirty minutes to an hour and he had no pulse or heart rate the whole time. The doctors agreed to call it and his family entered the room, leaning over him and gently rubbing his chest while saying his name. He quickly regained a pulse and consciousness.

Second Story: A patient came in coding and we worked on him and got nothing, so we brought in his wife to say goodbye and she began yelling at him at the top of her lungs and he returned. We arranged a transfer to a tertiary hospital and he coded again. She yells at him again and he returns again. They were then loading him into the helicopter and he coded again.

They then plan to have his wife fly alongside him in a helicopter to ensure she can scare him back to life if he coded again. The man survived, got a heart transplant, and is still alive to this day, all because his wife scared him back to life.

Ted Reyes - Euless, TX

I served as an overnight security guard in one of the country's biggest, richest, and oldest hospitals. My coworkers and I all have stories about one particular place, but the one I'll share is the one that happened to me.

This hospital was constructed in the late 1800's and served as the hospital's first psychiatric structure. As this was the late nineteenth century, little was really understood about mental conditions. Additionally, this hospital was well-known for its bizarre research. By combining these two statistics, one can deduce that some awful things were committed against these misunderstood psychiatric patients in this building. A few years before I began working protection there, this building had been converted into offices following the addition of a portion for an upgraded psychiatric ward to the newly constructed section of the hospital.

During my rounds that night, I happened to pass by said building. At night, this building was deserted, owing to its recent conversion to offices and the desire of the faculty who worked there to depart promptly at 9:00, if not earlier. They left their office doors open in some cases, which is a major violation given the presence of medical information in their offices. It was our responsibility to visit each floor to ensure that each door was closed, and if not, to secure it ourselves.

I conducted an initial sweep of the building to ensure it was safe, and then conducted my door checks. The hallways were fairly narrow, which allowed me to check both sides of the hallway's doors simultaneously. At the end of this corridor, you had to pass through two sets of doors to enter the final office, which was a dead end. Nothing was at risk.

I left the office's two sets of doors and stood transfixed by what I saw.

Each door was ajar; perfectly positioned so that their own weight did not cause them to close again. Additionally, one wheelchair was located at the end of said corridor, facing the stairs.

I had heard other security officers condemn that set of rounds outright due to strange activity occurring there, but I dismissed it until that night.

Since the former children's intensive care unit was then being converted into medical laboratories, we were required to patrol the area to ensure the area was safe, or to report on whether the contractor / foreman stayed overnight to prepare for the following day.

Several security officers have reported seeing a single child between the ages of five and eight with short brown hair while patrolling this location. Personally, I dismissed it as a tall tale told to scare me due to my inexperience at the time.

I was assigned to patrol the building one night, and a foreman who stayed late called security and requested an officer come up because "a child locked himself in a room, and I don't want him to get hurt with all the exposed wires."

For him, I unlocked the door. For about ten minutes, I examined what appeared to be a ten square foot space. No kid. I reported it as a false alarm and completed my patrol.

Along with another security officer, I was assigned to a special detail: a violent psych patient. In the middle of the night, he awoke, saw the other officer, and said hello.

When he saw me, he instantly began shouting at me, pleading with me not to hurt him. Though I am a very large gentleman (6'1 and 220 lbs), I make a conscious effort not to appear intimidating around psych patients in order to avoid escalating the situation.

He keeps pleading with me not to hurt him, and he promises that if I promise not to, he will arrange for something positive to happen to me. I promise, he will calm down and return to sleep, and I will forget about it.

The next day, I received a permanent collection of rounds and a decent promotion. Almost certainly a coincidence, but nonetheless intriguing.

A coworker security officer was making rounds in the aforementioned psychiatric facility. Heard a radio call for backup from one cop, in what could only be interpreted as a dry throat horror. Since I was close, I replied to his call, informing him that I was on my way. When I arrived, he had his head between his knees and was softly weeping next to a broken chandelier.

Now, had I not witnessed the strange occurrences in this area, I would have dismissed his testimony as nonsense. However, he believed that something kept him in place as the chandelier began spinning erratically until it began to fall. When it began to fall, he was "let go" and given permission to run, and jumped out of the way before it struck.

Tim Wells - Worthington, OH

PHOTOGRAPHS

I had been caring for an elderly woman who was alone since her husband died. She didn't talk much, but when she did, it was generally just random words. I felt terrible for her because so many of the people in her neighborhood with whom she seemed to enjoy spending time had passed away in just a short period of time since she arrived. She displayed a photograph of each of them alongside that of her husband and several others who were most likely family members in order to remember them. I had always felt sorry for her and lavished her with extra care, and we developed a strong bond. It seemed so unfair that she had such good fortune and continued to lose those she cared for. One day, she looked at me and said plainly, "Sweetie, I believe I'm finished now" before handing me a photograph.

It was a photograph of me, and I smiled because it warmed my heart that she thought so highly of me. She died about a week later, and I sobbed for days; it was devastating. She was aware that this was the end for her and made the most of her farewells.

I was speaking with a colleague less than two years later and she came up in conversation. My colleague referred to her as "that insane bitch," which appeared completely out of character for her, shocking and offending me profoundly. I conveyed this to her very bluntly, and she stared at me with this surprised expression and said, "Do you not know?" before explaining something to me that I was unaware of.

As it turned out, it was discovered shortly after her death that she poisoned her husband and that an investigation was launched because it looked as if she had a ritual of befriending someone, acquiring a photograph of them, concealing the photograph before she could kill them, usually by poisoning, and then showing the photograph as a sort of trophy. This was believed to be the cause of the increase in mortality rates during her visit, as well as the large number of photographs in her "collection." According to what I've read, the old "family" pictures had little to do with her, and the police were attempting to identify the individuals and compare them to other cold cases.

Sally Davis - Poland, OH

MAN IN THE HOSPITAL GOWN

I worked in an intensive care adult unit but was assigned to an evening shift with the children. It was after 10:00 PM, and all patients had retired to their rooms and beds. I overheard a boy crying and a mental health technician attempting to console him. I dashed to the room; the nine year old boy was inconsolable. He was crying, sweating, and trembling. He said that he saw something. He later told me that he saw a white man with gray hair in a hospital gown in his room after settling down. When we discussed what he saw, the child stood frozen in terror, tears streaming down his cheeks he said, "Miss, be still. Oh my God, he's following you."

We chose to approach "the man" and inform him that the small child was afraid.

The boy said that the man then turned around and walked away.

Within three minutes, a sixteen year old male at the end of the hall began crying. I dashed to his room and he was standing on his bed, attempting to flee a white man dressed in a hospital gown.

Joaquin Mack - Palm Springs, CA

My mother worked the night shift at a hospital in Arizona, in a border state, in a historically significant mining town. She's working her night shift, moving from room to room, when an elderly lady who walked the halls due to insomnia informed her that some strange goat man was constantly attempting to enter through the gate. My mother was unconcerned, but she is a devout Catholic and had some moments of quiet prayer to herself.

After a few seconds, there was a shriek; she couldn't put her finger on what it was, but it was a terrible shriek that made the blood turn to ice. She then proceeded to the nurses station to inquire if someone else had heard that, which they had. The shriek was heard throughout the hospital. Everyone was terrified, particularly religious women and men. A few of them go to the windows and see hoof prints next to the doors and windows, with no trail leading towards or away from the building.

My tale was very unsettling. I, too, became a CNA and worked nights in a secure dementia and Alzheimer's facility. I've had bizarre moments, however this one will always be with me.

I was finishing up my binders when a light went off out of the hall, so I took it, punched my code in and went out since the other CNA was busy with someone else. I went in, asking if everything was OK. Sleepily, my little lady tells me there's a darn woman who keeps knocking on her window wanting to come in, and that she really wants to go back to sleep. She insists I go and let her in, and I'm thinking to myself, this sounds all too familiar. I reassure her, peer out the window, and there is nothing there. Maybe she was dreaming, and really tired and mistook it as her room mate.

Following the incident, I return to my unit. Sit, eat a snack, converse with my head nurse, talk with my daily insomniacs; and it is now about 3:00 AM. A light goes off, and in my unit. Also, this unit has no outbound lines at all. I head down the hall, and ask if all is OK. My lady says she can't sleep, someone keeps banging on her window and she is scared. I again reassure the lady thinking about what just happened. I told my nurse and she laughed and said "This has been happening for years."

Daniel Jones - Los Angeles, CA

PUPPY

I'm a certified nursing assistant who has been work-ing night shifts in hospitals for seven years and I have quite a few tales. I arrived at work one night and Jen, one of the nurses, informed me and my coworker Jay of the most bizarre event that had occurred a few hours ago. A patient had suddenly passed away in one of the halls. The room was cleaned and soon occupied by another patient who had coded, was pronounced dead, but was brought back to life. He complained to the nurse shortly after being admitted to his bed, "I can't be in here. This man will not stop staring at me. He's genuinely concerned for his puppy. His dog is un-aware that he's dead." She had thought he was delu-sory and said, "Oh yeah? What does he look like?" He accurately identified the deceased patient. As it turns out, the man did own a puppy. The new admission was relocated to a different room.

"I'm not a believer," Jay said. "I'd like to see. Tonight, I'm gonna provoke him." At 3 AM, all three of us were at the nursing station. Jay began playing YouTube vid-eos containing a variety of puppy sounds. We quickly forget what we're doing and engage in another dis-cussion after two lift team members arrive. Suddenly, everybody but Jay hears it. "Stop!" Coming from the empty room.

Ashley Digirolamo - Saint Louis, MO

PINK

When I worked in a nursing home, the levels were connected by an elevator, with stairs at the far end. It was shaped like a U, with the nurses station at one end and the residents spread out around the unit, allowing you to see all exits and apprehend any confused residents. Since I was pursuing a career as a registered nurse at the time, I was still on night shift. The elevator would randomly travel from the top to the bottom floor and then return about an hour later to the floor you were on.

I didn't think much about it, assuming it was a machine quirk or something. That is, before I encountered her, the lady in pink.

I was studying in the nurse's station when I noticed what seemed to be a resident wearing pink and walking without her walker from her room on the opposite end of the unit to the elevator. As a good nurse, I ran to prevent her from tripping or falling. When I arrived, she was not there. Thus, I entered her room and discovered that the sides of her bed were raised and she was asleep.

As I walk back, I note the call button is illuminated. The elevator door opens, the elevator door closes, and the elevator begins to move without anyone inside.

The next morning, I inform my colleagues, who inform me that it's the lady in pink. They tell me they had this enormous Samoan man who worked nights for two weeks before he saw the lady in pink and then left. I resigned and obtained employment as a security guard in a maximum-security psychiatric hospital.

Donna Silvas - Beckley, WV

COWBOY

My mother was a registered nurse in a small western town. This hospital was linked to a senior living facility, and the RN was in charge of both sides of the building at night; hospital and living home. Usually, she worked as the overnight RN and was assisted by one or two CNAs. She encountered this apparition about six or seven times during her ten year tenure there, and everyone referred to it as "The Man in Black." Each experience was similar, with the exception of the building's location.

Throughout the night, she was required to perform her rounds and would have to walk around a corner from the nurses' station/ER to the hospital's beds and the senior home. She would see the apparition immediately after turning a corner or immediately after exiting one room and entering the next. She would see the same apparition outside the next room. The apparition was of a man dressed in a worn black cowboy suit, worn black cowboy boots, and a worn black cowboy hat.

The most unsettling aspect of this man's appearance was his lack of definition in his face. She described it as though a man's face had been drawn with charcoal and slightly smeared, resulting in a slight blurring. He stood about 6'5" and towered over her. However, whenever she saw him, whether ten or three feet away, he would stop and look at her before turning and walking into the room he was outside of. When she entered the room, there would be no other occupants or anything out of place. The first few times frightened her into a panic, but she gradually continued without allowing herself to be terrified. However, this man brought additional attention to the patient.

In about 90% of all cases observed by other RNs, the patient's health deteriorated within a few days and the patient most often died shortly afterwards. As a result, if the overnight RN encountered "The Man in Black," additional measures were taken for that patient. Another strange aspect of the apparition is that it is still seen by the RN alone. No CNA has directly seen the apparition. My mother still maintained that he knew who would be the most capable of assisting at the moment. On the other hand, I interpreted it exactly the opposite way. I always assumed it was almost to taunt the RNs, as he would inform them of impending events but leave them powerless to prevent them. Even though I am not an RN, it always creeps me out if she points out where she has seen him.

Nancy Horton - Racine, WI

THIN

Each night, prior to the start of the next shift, I check on all my patients, make sure their briefs are clean, and refill their water pitchers. This occurs usually shortly after sunset. Three distinct patients in three distinct rooms have expressed fear of the tall, thin man in the corner, pointing directly over my shoulder.

Tony Bain - Southfield, MI

LONELY

I work on a pediatric bone marrow transplant unit, and unfortunately, we lose a significant number of children. Since our children are here for longer periods of time, typically 1-6 months for inpatient care, we must move them between rooms to keep it clean.

One specific three year old boy receives no visits from relatives. He seldom interacts well with workers and would sometimes mutter to himself. We relocated him to a room where a small child had recently died and began finding him conversing with various locations in the room and staring and nodding while alone. Then he began using new phrases, despite the fact that he had not seen a rise in visitors.

My colleagues are sure he's communicating with the little girl who died there, and while I'm a fairly skeptic, I always get the creeps when I walk by and see him conversing with himself.

Margie Tyler - Longview, TX

VISITOR

I work in a level one trauma center that serves eleven counties, implying a fair amount of carnage routinely. I was alone in the bay one morning between 3 and 4 AM, catching up on paperwork. We have four trauma bays and two resuscitation rooms arranged in a rectangle around a nursing station. I became aware of a man approaching me from behind, outside the nursing station and into one of the trauma rooms. I had not heard any big noisy motion activated doors open and he glanced back at me as he passed through the room doors, but did not respond when I called out, "Hello?"

I walked around to ensure it wasn't a misplaced visitor and that no one was present. There is no way out except through the entrance, which was out of my line of sight for just a split second.

I later told another nurse about the story and the fear I had when searching for the weird fellow. She mentioned that she had a similar experience the previous week. Occasionally, it is brought up, the same story. The same guy enters the room and then exits before you can find him. We've chosen to simply ignore him. I hope he does, however, find what he is searching for.

Jose Manning - Rushville, NE

HALLUCINATIONS

I was working a night shift, supervising one patient who was experiencing hallucinations.

This patient had a routine in which he desired to go out for a cigarette every hour. I wheeled him out for a cigarette, which seemed to exacerbate his hallucinations. I had been escorting this patient many times during the night. Around 12 AM, I escorted him outside for his last cigarette before bed.

While outside, he inquired as to whether I could see a tiny boy attempting to escape the locked cage in front of us. As I did for all of his hallucinations, I said no; this seemed to help minimize the duration of their appearance.

He then told me that he could see a man and a dog running towards us, despite the fact that it was the dead of night and there was no one else in the hospital; there was no man or dog. However, when the automatic doors fifty feet behind us opened without anyone present, I began to doubt that they were hallucinations. I quickly returned us to the ward after that.

Anita Chapman - Springfield, MA

HAND WASHER

My mother received her nursing training in the 1950s at London's old Westminster Teaching Hospital. She was making rounds in the children's ward during one of her first night shifts. All was fine, the children were asleep, but she noticed the sink faucet running in one of the rooms, which was strange because it had been fine when she had been by a few minutes ago. She thought one of the children had gotten up and was thirsty or something, so she turned it off and continued her rounds.

When her shift ended, she checked out with the Matron, who inquired as to whether she had any concerns. She said that there was nothing except for a faucet that had been left on in one of the rooms. The Matron was shocked and said, "Oh no!" She then told her that the ward was plagued by a ghost that washed its hands, while still running the faucet, whenever a child was about to die.

My mother dismissed this, stating that none of the children in the ward were severely ill, and returned home. When she returned to work the next evening, she learned that a previously healthy child in that room had suffered a sudden seizure and died just hours after she discovered the open faucet.

Kevin Cuevas - Boca Raton, FL

IT WAS KNOCKING

My previous employer had a geriatric facility. I floated to assist one night and was informed that all patients put in a particular room at the end of the hall would experience the same "hallucinations" of a tall man dressed in a suit and another of a baby in a baby carriage outside the room.

In my unit, a general medicine/surgery unit, a patient had died the previous evening in a room that was now vacant. The call light for that room stayed on all night, even after we unplugged it from the wall, until we went into the room and asked, "Can I assist you?"

My unit was configured in the form of a plus sign, with the nurse station in the middle. One of the wings was sealed off by double doors because it had been renovated as a gastroenterology clinic where patients could undergo colonoscopies and other procedures. On night shift, on the same medical / surgery unit, we heard a heavy knocking from those double doors, as if someone was locked out and attempting to gain access to the nurse's station. One of my colleagues walked over and noticed that nobody was standing on the other side of the entrance, and that all the lights had been switched off. It continued to happen, banging loudly. We also summoned the security guard to investigate, but he was nowhere to be found.

Occasionally, I'd have to pass through the empty GI clinic in order to reach another elevator or section of the hospital, and occasionally, I'd walk into heavy "clouds" of perfume in the empty vacant corridor, which had been empty for some time.

That hospital dates all the way back to the 1930s, and since working there, I've developed a strong belief in ghosts and the supernatural.

Tom Fine - Paducah, KY

LTC NURSING

LTC nursing is an excellent environment for seeing strange things. There was the church lady "prophetess" who regularly informed girls of their pregnancies and inquired about my personal life. There was the room that sometimes went completely dark, with no light visible for a minute or two. There was the room where three consecutive residents screamed about the child killer. There was the patient who kept asking us to assist "the old guy" and perfectly identified the previous patient. He passed away several weeks before she was admitted. There is the constant squeak of shoes in the Alzheimer's unit, random cries, and chairs that rock on their own.

Donna Presnell - Newark, NJ

BATH TUB

When I was working in a long-term care facility, I was walking down the hall conversing with a CNA when we suddenly heard the noisy sound of running water in the toilet. Since all of the patients were already in bed, I turned to her and asked, "What is that?" We walked over to the bathroom, which was only accessible via key, unlocked the door, and entered. We switched on the lights because they were out.

The tub water was flowing at full speed into the tub, despite the fact that no one was in it. I went over and completely switched off the faucet.

I asked why the water was running while everyone was in bed. The CNA stated that odd things occur frequently in that bathroom and on the floor, including lights turning on and off and objects moving around or turning on in that bathroom.

What's strange is that I heard the water turn on while standing near that toilet, despite the fact that no one had entered, and the handle had to be turned completely to the right to turn it off.

Audrey Jones - Atlanta, GA

I was operating in an intensive care unit. I had a patient who would repeat everything said to her and stayed with her the whole night. When I entered the room, she began telling me about all the ways she died. "I died of a narcotic overdose, I died of an insulin overdose, I died on a sunny Sunday afternoon," and so forth. Later, she raised her eyes to the ceiling and said, "They're all still there." I dashed out of that room as quickly as possible.

Another time, I had a blind patient who constantly inquired about the time in the night. When I went into his room to check on him, he said to me, "It's the witching hour." The time was 3:33 AM.

Catherin Burnes - Kailua, HI

Around 1:30 AM, I had a patient admitted to a room. He was alert and well-informed. He was wheeled into the emergency room on an ER gurney and immediately began freaking out about "him." Did we not see "him"? He will not remain in that space and that he wants to get as far away from it as possible. We adjust his room assignment and assist him in settling in. Later that morning, I inquired as to who "he" is. It states that the room must be exorcised. "He" seems to be a very angry dead man in his mid-40's.

He was displeased to have another man in "his" bed. The room was perpetually freezing either in the winter or summer. The lights used to switch on for no apparent reason.

Ted James - Providence, RI

HUSBAND

I served as a night shift aide in a long-term care facility about 14 years ago. I was assigned to a hall I had never served before. It was about 1 AM when I saw an elderly gentleman exit a bed, walk down the corridor, and exit the facility. When I entered that room, I discovered that the resident was awake. When I inquired as to who she was speaking with, she informed me that her husband often visited her late at night. I approached the other aide on the floor and was informed that the resident was 102 years old and her husband had been deceased for about thirty years.

William Angel - El Mirage, CA

SHE HAS ONE OF THESE

I used to work at Cincinnati Children's, and there is a little girl who appears at the bedside of dying children the day before they die and assures them that all will be fine. They even mentioned her during orientation.

We had a patient move in surgery in Indy at a children's hospital, but her room was haunted. One night, a small African American boy saw her and said, "she looks like me and has one of these and one of these," referring to his central line and GT. Additionally, she possessed a central line and a GT.

Bobbie Morris - Middle River, MN

SURGEON

I was called in one night for a bad case in the OR and we were in the middle of it when I saw a guy dressed as a surgeon walk past the OR door and head down the hall towards a dead end. We were at the end of the hall. I went to the door and couldn't see anybody, yelled "Hello" and still no one. I had learned that the operating room was haunted by the ghost of a surgeon.

Gail Masters - Arlington Heights, IL

I worked in a long-term care facility where a sweet little guy would be clear over on one side of a twin bed and when I asked him to scoot over so he wouldn't fall off, he said he didn't want to disturb the little girl lying next to him. I'm guessing there were once children in this place. Residents in the same hall would see a lady in black entering rooms, and within a day or two, the resident would die.

Lee Seely - Evansville, WI

GIGGLES

One night, about 1 a.m., I was eating alone in the cafeteria. When I stepped out into the hallway to catch the elevator, I overheard a small child laughing. Nobody was in the vicinity. I requested security to walk around and check; all that was down there was EVS with the doors closed, nowhere near that corridor.

Jeffrey Craven - Norcross, GA

MY ENERGY

When I posted on Facebook that my bedroom lights
kept coming on and off, a friend who "sees things"
said it was a recently deceased little boy. Unbeknown
to her, I'd worked in hem-onc that week and a little
boy had died just before my shift. A few days later,
I was taking a picture of a curtain I'd made in my
daughter's room and there were two orbs dancing on
my screen. My friend said one of them was the boy.
She said he liked my energy.

Ricardo Moye - Philadelphia, PA

The facility I worked at was built on the site of a former playground. In the 1930s, a small child died there. Residents who were blind or suffering from Alzheimer's disease would often "see" a small child. They often identified the same child dressed identically.

I had a dementia-stricken ninety year old resident who hadn't talked in years. She was on the verge of death. "All right, I'll see you tomorrow," she said as she glanced behind me. "I love you." She was pronounced dead exactly 24 hours later.

A resident never used her own bathroom for a bowel movement. She was constantly going to the room across the hall. After she died, witnesses claimed to see someone enter the room across from hers. And years later, from individuals who were unaware of the story.

John Foster - Dublin, CA

NATIVES

Navajo, Zuni, and Hopi Natives work and visit the GIMC hospital where I work. The skins walkers are the most frequently mentioned. Additionally, the floor on which I work is undoubtedly haunted. I heard computer keys typing in one room. I was alone in the lobby. I got up to investigate the source of the noise and the noise ceased. I sat back, and it resumed. I asked a coworker, and she freaked out and confirmed that it was an old coworker who used to do her Master's homework in that room. She was fatally injured in a freak traffic crash.

Everyone seems to have heard the machine keys and recognized them as well, as I mentioned room 9 another day and they said "It's her again." The floor is haunted by ghosts of small children and a surgeon, and moaning can be heard from room 5. I heard and thought I saw a small child near room 5 and believed a patient was in the room 1 night but discovered no one was there. I was terrified.

Bernice Provost - Tucson, AZ

CALL

When I was a PCA, I worked at Mercy Hospital in Mount Airy. We always had strange things happen, but the best was one night when my unit received a random call from a room on the floor below us. On the fourth floor, one area had been closed for an extended period of time and was deserted. On the other side of the floor, there was a small treatment facility. We received this call when no one was on the floor. I and a few others descended the stairs and made our way to that side of the floor. We located the room and entered to discover it was empty. It was being used for storage, and the space lacked a call light or phone. Nobody could account for it.

Apart from that, we had call lights that automatically turned off when no one was in the area. We simply assumed it was a ghost.

Sheila Goode - Cincinnati, OH

ALL RIGHT

For a prolonged period of time, I was assigned to night duty in the hospital. I was forced to jot down each patient's name one night after noticing a patient I hadn't seen in a few weeks. When I contemplated the possibility that he had been transferred to our surgical hospital, I felt odd. He met my gaze and smiled as I maintained an as-if-everything-were-fine face. It was unexpected to see him in his best light as opposed to the one I remember. However, I was unable to find his name on the patient census when I entered my notes. I looked for him using his given name and was astounded to learn that he had died two days before. I imagine he returned to tell us that he was all right.

Lee Merchant - Chicago, IL

OVERSEER

At the district hospital where I previously worked, it was very common for us staff nurses to see a lady dressed in white walking down the corridor in the early morning hours and patients did as well. We just lost one of our nursing supervisors; she died suddenly. Our emergency room call light often goes out when no one is in or near the room. We are both convinced that this is our supervisor checking in.

While making my rounds as a new RN on a unit, I noticed an elderly woman dressed in a hospital gown. Assuming she was lost or unable to sleep, I signaled her from afar to inquire as to what was wrong. Grabbing her attention, she turned her face to me, grinned, and entered a patient's room through a wall! I was made immobile by what I saw. I later discovered that the woman had died three days before in a car crash while supervising her husband who was hospitalized in the room she entered.

John Williams - Baton Rouge, LA

BREEZE

I was working a night shift when the call light for room 250 went off. For all I know, this room is empty, so I attempted to switch off the desk lamp but it would not turn off. I made my way down to the room to double check. When I entered the room, I heard a rattling sound coming from the window, as if something or someone was attempting to escape. Knowing what could happen, I summoned all my courage and took a deep breath, turned on the lights, and walked over to the window, which I opened. I felt strange as a gentle breeze passed by and flew past me and out the window. I later discovered that a patient had died during the morning and that the nurses prior to my shift had somehow neglected to open the doors. As strange as it sounds, when anyone passes, allow them to leave and open the room's windows!

Jerry Carr - Chicago, IL

While in college, I worked the night shift alone at one of the country's oldest nursing homes. I have a lot of stories to share, but this one permanently altered my demeanor. I was about to get extra linen for a room when I sneezed and heard a plain as day "Bless you" from behind me.

I was about to begin a prayer when to my surprise a voice whispered near my ear, "Our Father in heaven."

From then on, I had to restrain myself from sneezing and abstained from reciting The Lord's Prayer for an extended period of time.

Rudolf Rocha - Lake Charles, LA

INTRUDER

I worked as a registry nurse on the night shift, and it was a very quiet and peaceful time at 3 AM. When doing basic floor rounds, I sensed something behind me and turned around to see a mysterious girl figure dressed in a hospital gown running into a residents room. Despite knowing the plot, I was not afraid. I was thinking of her as an intruder. As I entered the bed, the resident was awake and asked, "Did you see that?"

I asked, "What," and the resident responded "She went in there", pointing to the closed bathroom. I waited a moment and then called for assistance to ensure there was no intruder and that the device was clear. I can't describe it to this day, but I know what I saw and, strangely enough, what my patient saw in her mental state.

Melissa Thomsen - Plainfield, IL

BALLOONS

It was my second year operating in the hospital as a registered nurse, and I was assigned to a pediatric unit on the night shift. Frequently, our patients were nursery and elementary school students. We had a patient who insisted on visitors always bringing balloons when they paid her a visit. She passed away earlier this month after a lengthy hospitalization. After a few days, one of my coworkers celebrated her birthday, and we decorated the station with some balloons. We saw two balloons bobbing up and down slowly in the air. This would not have worried me except that those balloons then came to a halt in front of the girl's previous room and slowly made their way back into the nurse's station. Air currents cannot account for this.

Heather Carter - Blue Springs, MO

CRASH

I was reminded of my own experience working in a hospital in Japan. I was doing a 12-hour shift. The main nurses' office is closed, and keys are only available to RNs, LPNs, and administration. The nurses' station where I was stationed was directly next to the building, and it was precisely 3 AM when I heard a loud crash emanating from the office. The next day, I discovered that a filing cabinet had collapsed and papers were strewn across the room. The windows were closed, the door was shut, and the air conditioning was turned off.

Steven Cobb - Kissimmee, FL

I used to work as a nurse's aide in a nursing home and was reminded of a coworker who had a strange encounter. She was attempting to check on a patient who was a Nun one night. According to her, a group of nuns entered the room but made no attempt to speak with her, with the exception of one with whom she made eye contact. However, no one else on the floor was aware of the nuns' arrival or departure. According to legend, the hospital was constructed on the site of an old convent that was destroyed by fire in the late 1800's.

Chris Ducote - Mount Pleasant, SC

Prior to this, I worked in an outmoded labor and distribution factory. Due to the small size of the hospital, I often returned alone. Due to my preference for dim lighting and a serene environment back there, I naturally heard a lot of creeps and groans. There was an entire back hallway that was unoccupied, and it was also inaccessible to anyone who passed me. I could hear metal items clanging together and doors closing. Someone appeared to be ready for a cesarean section. There always seemed to be something about me. There was also a back area on the med / surg floor that was never used. It had been converted from a patient room to a storage area. That room was strange. The call light was flashing incessantly, and nobody was in the vicinity. The entire hospital radiated an eerie aura. Perhaps the adjacent cemetery was the source.

Maria Haack - Wheaton, IL

I work in a long-term care facility, and we have received several reports from patients that they saw a small child. This boy enters their rooms, switches on and off their call lights, and throws stuff on the floor. This building was formerly used as an orphanage. Additionally, there are tales of an old-fashioned nurse dressed all in white and wearing a white hat that would be seen walking down the hall late at night doing a bed check and would enter someone's room and linger for a few minutes if they were gravely ill or on the verge of death. I suppose one aide saw her a while ago and declined to go down that hall for a week, and the person whose room she went into recently returned from the hospital, still very ill.

We have seen a white figure in the pharmacy room, and sometimes the carts are pushed down the hall when you are in a room administering medications. Several times, one of the male CNAs mentioned seeing a very tall black figure moving from room to room. We have all seen spinning balls of light. According to what we have deduced from old photographs of the land on which the nursing home is located, there was a mobile home park on one end and a cemetery on the other. Everyone has seen a small child wandering around, but the most bizarre sight was when they saw wet children's footsteps coming down the hall and followed them to the wall, where they discovered footprints in the snow outside that led directly to that spot in the wall.

Dwight Brown - Camden, NJ

CARL

I once heard a report about a fifth-floor neuro unit. This was relayed to me by the first person. The nurse was at the desk when a gentleman dressed in white nursing garb entered through the double doors, walked into an empty office, and never returned.

The nurse thought it was strange and entered the bed, which was empty.

He approached the double doors and opened them to find two resp techs conversing at the entrance. They swore they'd been there the whole time and that nobody had entered through the doors.

When one of his coworkers returned from lunch and he informed her of what had occurred, she was astounded. "That's Carl. He worked here as a LVN years ago and was charged with child molestation. He was certain he was about to be arrested and jumped out the window of that room to commit suicide. We see him often."

Jerry Hill - Fresno, CA

MY FRIEND DEE

On the other side of the curtain, Dee had just been floated to an old hospital's emergency room. Normally, it was very busy, but that particular night, everything went swimmingly and the patients were calm.

Dee was checking on one of her sleeping patients when she noticed her nape hairs standing on end. She sensed a presence on the other side of the curtain, right behind her. There was nobody there, and Dee chalked it up to her imagination.

It happened again a few minutes later, in a different room. Dee felt a curious paralysis and her hackles grew. She was once again aware of a heavy presence beside her, and although she could see a silhouette in the curtain inches away, she couldn't see the other person's shoes. She immediately heard an echoing high pitched giggle, and the darkness vanished, allowing her to breathe normally once more.

Later, the other nurses shared how they, too, had brief moments where they sensed someone watching them, but not nearly as strongly as Dee had.

Kevin Baxter - Reston, VA

I was employed by a large hospital in the suburbs that had stood since the Second World War. There was one space that was still vacant at the end of the night because any patient who stayed there complained about seeing a nurse in a rocking chair.

According to their accounts, the nurse never looked them in the eyes and only swayed softly while gazing out the window. It was allegedly a nun who served in the hospital during the war, and the window she often looked out of overlooked the hospital's old cemetery.

I never believed the stories until one night when all the beds were occupied and they were forced to place a young patient in that room. As I checked in on the young girl in the morning, he found that she seemed to have a restless night. Further probing revealed that the young girl had said, "The old nurse in my room was really sad. She spent the whole night rocking beside me."

Kenneth Haywood - Holts Summit, MO

SHADOW ON THE WALL

I was a nurse caring for a terminally ill male patient. Throughout my night shift, the patient became increasingly distressed, and I attempted to relax and comfort him. It initially worked, but it occurred again, leaving the patient much more terrified than before. Since the patient was unintelligible, I was unable to comprehend what was happening.

I walked over to the deserted nurses' station directly across from the patient's bed, leaving the door open. I was startled to see an unmistakable black shadow hunched menacingly over the patient's anxious body as he looked back idly.

After a moment, it vanished and the patient died that night.

Mary Hunt - Shreveport, LA

My friend Helen had a patient who was very attractive. He was, however, very cantankerous, and after a while, the nurses began to roll their eyes when he was listed, except for Helen, who possessed saintly patience.

As a result, the handsome patient enjoyed tormenting Helen and mocked and annoyed her to varying degrees. He was hospitalized for an extended period of time due to complications.

Helen took a detour to the bathroom before her shift one night after returning from a rest day. After washing her hands, Helen raised her eyes and saw her patient's handsome face mirrored clearly in the bathroom mirror. He was maniacally laughing, as if taunting her. She was shocked and turned quickly to reprimand him, only to discover herself alone in the tiny tiled bathroom.

Helen's mind was blown later when she learned that her handsome patient had died the night before. For several weeks afterwards, Helen avoided all mirrors, especially at night.

Laurine Byrnes - Bloomingburg, NY

My friend Jill explained her encounter with a possession to me.

A patient was afflicted with a variety of ailments. Many patients are fearful of death, but he stood out significantly. When his monitors beeped warnings, he would yell at the nurses, "Do not let me die! Please do not let me die!"

Jill and the other nurses later discovered why he was so upset.

At 2:00 AM., the man's cardiac monitor begins to alert V-Tach. Jill and another nurse rushed to his bed, Jill trailing closely behind due to her position as the crash cart's driver. She ran into the first nurse, who had become very pale. When she raised her eyes to the bed, she noticed their patient was sitting two inches above it. He laughed with a wicked expression on his lips. "You idiots aren't going to let me die, are you?" he asked.

He continued to chuckle, and Jill said how they had been frozen in place. Nonetheless, she activated Code Blue, and their patient went onto V-fib, collapsing back into the bed as he did so. After thirty minutes, the nurses began coding him.

Five minutes later, as the team is washing up, the dead man unexpectedly sits up. He said, maniacally laughing, "You let him die." Their patient abruptly screamed in agony, and everyone later heard whispers of "do not let me die."

"The night shift nurses held a prayer service in the break room before we left for home," Jill told me "Afterwards, we all had nightmares for weeks."

Mitchell Bradshaw - Raleigh, NC

DOPPELGANGER

Our next story involves a nurse, but not a patient. A new nurse was assigned to a department who had a slightly different vibe from the other new nurses. For some odd cause, she stood out, and the others immediately felt uneasy in her presence.

A seasoned nurse was highly critical of the new nurses. She overheard a new nurse confiding in another new nurse about her ability to "see" things and having odd things happen to her.

The veteran nurse confronted her in front of the others for spewing such nonsense, and the young nurse burst into tears. Forgetting about the incident, the experienced nurse entered the nurses' sleeping quarters a few nights later and saw the young nurse's sleeping form and a second form of the same individual sitting up and staring at her.

The veteran nurse slowly backed away and dashed to the nurses station. Later, the new nurse revealed that her family often received reports of her being seen in locations she did not frequent.

Marjorie Velasco - Okeechobee, FL